KT-143-334

THE
WIND
IN THE
WILLOWS

First published in 1985
This edition published in 1986 by
Octopus Books Limited
59 Grosvenor Street
London W1

by arrangement with Thames Television Limited

Illustration – Beverly Bush
Jacket designer – Mike Watts
Designed by Design 23
Art Editor – Ronnie Wilkinson
Editor – Carol Watson

ISBN 0 86273 259 X

Printed in New Zealand

A recorded tone on the story tape is used to indicate
when a page should be turned.

CONTENTS

ALFRED AND THE CARAVAN

The autumn promised a good harvest: blackberries shone from the tangles of briars, rowans and hawthorns were laden, handfuls of elderberries dangled from sagging branches, and the farmer's fields were now shimmering gold in the September sun. Ratty and Mole were to be found, on this glorious morning, equipped for the road with knapsacks, sturdy boots and stout sticks, striding along through the richness. A little way behind, and *not* striding – indeed resting at the roadside – was a weary and footsore Toad.

'Oh, do stop! Do stop!' he pleaded.

'My dear Toad, we stopped two minutes back!' expostulated Rat.

'Yes, yes! I know! I can't help it if my wretched straps keep slipping!' Toad argued.

'You shouldn't have tried to carry so much!' Rat retorted.

'So much? There's hardly anything! Smoked salmon, calves' foot jelly, stuffed olives, lemon curd, fruit cake, two peaches, a packet of rich tea biscuits and half a bottle of champagne. I don't call *that* a lot!'

'Oh, Toad! If we *keep* stopping, we'll never get anywhere!'

'But we've already got *here*! From *Toad Hall*!'

'My dear Toad, it can't be more than three-quarters of a mile!' Ratty exclaimed in reply.

'Three-quarters of a mile ... Oh! No *wonder* I feel tired! Whoever wanted to go hiking in the first place?'

'You did Toad!' said Mole, matter-of-factly, over Toad's protestations. '"Fresh air's the thing," you said!'

'I say – I do dislike a fellow who throws a chap's words back in his face,' replied the unabashed Toad.

The Rat considered. 'Well, Toad, if your new-found enthusiasm for hiking has burnt itself out already, what *do* you want to do?'

'Nothing!' Toad snapped back defiantly.

A new voice joined in. 'That's all as some of us *has* to do!'

Ratty started: 'Hullo! Who's . . . ? Oh! Hullo, Alfred!' And indeed it was Alfred, their faithful companion from the days of the open road and the canary-coloured caravan.

Unlike the Rat, Mole had taken in what Alfred had said. 'All some of us has – er, *have* – to do? How do you mean, Alfred?'

Alfred snorted in reply, and tossed his head towards the next-door field. 'Huh! Hear that!?'

Toad hadn't time for such a leisurely discussion – unless it involved him:

'Yes, yes! It sounds like a goods train.'

Alfred wasn't to be diverted; ''arvester! That's what the noise is. A 'arvester!'

Rat couldn't see the connection.

'Erm – I don't think I quite ...'

'It's the farmer! Him an' his new-fangled machines! Ain't good enough to have me pulling the mower like what I've always done! 'As to get a mechanical 'arvester! Huh!'

Mole was concerned: 'Oh, dear! So what are you ...?'

'Nothing! Nothing to do till ploughing do start again! Ain't as if Mr Toad has a caravan for me to pull!'

Toad had forgotten his earlier passion. But caravans had wheels! They were easier than hiking! But he didn't want to give away his motives, and, 'Oh, yes! The caravan!' was all he allowed himself to say.

Mole was more enthusiastic. 'Oh, I loved the caravan!' A snatch of their song came back to him: 'It's a life of ease on the Open Road ...'

Rat joined in: 'Rambling where you please on the Open Road ...' But both stopped short when they heard Alfred remark casually: 'Still there.'

'I'm sorry, Alfred?' said the surprised rat.

'It's still there – just up there.'

'Oh, I say, *do* let's see!' Mole was captivated by the prospect. And so was Toad – even if his reasons were a little different.

He was determined to demonstrate to his friends just how much he had revelled in those days. 'The journeys we took in her – remember? Those weeks of slothful pleasure?'

The Rat was not to be beguiled. 'No!'

That was not the answer Toad expected. 'Ah ha! Yes, ... No! No?'

'You used it for just three days – and then you took up motoring!' Undaunted by this home-truth, Toad enthused over the abandoned caravan, stuck in a ditch in the field corner.

Mole was still enraptured in his memories. 'It would be wonderful to travel the open road again!' he enthused.

'Mm! You weren't pulling 'er!' Alfred retorted.

Mole was horrified by his thoughtlessness. 'Oh! No! I'm sorry, Alfred. I forgot!'

But Alfred had been only half-serious in his complaint. 'Be better than doing nothing,' he said.

By now, Toad's enthusiasm had been totally rekindled. 'My friends, we'll do it,' he announced. 'She *shall* be restored! We *shall* travel the world – and not on foot! We *shall* explore the

ever-changing scenery, live the Romany life ...'

But he was cut short in the midst of his oratory. It was the Fieldmice:

'Quick! We'd better get help! We'll have to ...' And three of them scuttled through the hedge from the next-door field. 'Oh, Mr Alfred! It's the harvester! It's mowed our homes!'

Rat was horrified: 'Mowed your homes! Oh my gosh!'

'I knew no good'd come of new-fangled ideas!' Alfred remarked gloomily.

Toad, for all his self-centred talk, was the most generous animal in a crisis – if sometimes a little impractical. 'My poor dear chaps!' he exclaimed. 'Homeless! Well, you'll just have to stay at Toad Hall!'

The Fieldmice were delighted with this ready offer of help, but it wasn't quite the help they needed. 'Please sir, that's very kind of you, but ... well, we're not used to *big* houses! No!'

'Well then *my* home will suit you very well!' Mole asserted.

'Yes, but there isn't just us, Mr Mole!' replied the spokesman.

'How do you mean?' asked the mystified Rat.

'Well, er ... you see ...' He whistled through his teeth, and a dozen or so other mice appeared. Mole understood the reason for the Fieldmouse's hesitation.

'Oh dear! Oh dear! There wouldn't be room for *half* of them!'

'Not even if some stayed with me!' agreed Rat.

The disappointed Fieldmice broke into a chatter: 'Oh dear!' They were silenced by Alfred clearing his throat purposefully.

'Ahem!'

'Sorry, Alfred!' Ratty prompted.

'Caravan.'

Mole and Ratty did not immediately follow Alfred's thinking and Mole began, 'I don't think we should be bothering with that when ...'

'Why can't they stay in *that* for a night or two?' Alfred explained.

'Oh, Mr Alfred, that would be wonderful!' said the delighted Fieldmice.

'It would have to be mended ...' Mole put in, his usual practical self.

'Well, we could help you mend it!' said one Fieldmouse, and the others cheered their approval.

'That's jolly decent of you!' Toad enthused, foreseeing some hard work being done for him.

Alfred set off to fetch some ropes; Toad began to show the Fieldmice round their new home, extolling its merits like an estate agent with a *particularly* desirable residence. 'It has, of course, everything that you could wish for ...'

'... except a wheel.' Rat interposed quietly.

'Except a *wheel*!?'

'There's one missing! Look!' Rat pointed to the bare axle.

'Please, sir! It's our roundabout,' explained a Fieldmouse. 'It must have come off and rolled onto the roadside, Mr Toad ...'

'Ha! Well now it's going to be a wheel again!' He turned to his friends. 'Leave this to me!' he

commanded. Indicating some half of the Fieldmice with a grandiose sweep of his hand, he continued, 'Erm . . . ! Ten or a dozen of you mice! Follow me!' And he marched off with his army, just as Alfred returned with the ropes.

So the next hour or so was filled with shouts and cries – of instructions, of effort, of satisfaction as things were done. 'Shall I tie this here?' 'Right, ho!' . . . 'Look out, young Billy!' And finally, as it came clear 'Hurray!'

Toad, meanwhile, had managed, with much effort from his little helpers and rather less actual work from himself, to get the recalcitrant wheel upright. He attempted to reunite it with the caravan by rolling it along, like a giant hoop, and all nearly ended in disaster when it gathered speed and threatened to run down Toad, who had somehow contrived to get in front. But Mole saved the situation by ramming a stick through the spokes, felling the wheel not too far from where it was needed.

Toad appeared shaken by his experience: 'Oh dear, Oh dear!'

Ratty considered. Was Toad really so unnerved by the near-mishap? 'Better catch your breath, Toad,' he remarked, non-commitally, 'before we get back to work.'

Toad pulled out his watch. 'Good heavens! Is that the time?

I'd no idea! I shall miss my appointment!'

'Appointment, Toad?' said Rat, suspiciously. 'You never mentioned an appointment!'

'Well it went clean out of my head! Must rush!'

'Dear me! *Now* what's he up to?' mused Rat, largely to himself. 'No steadiness, that's Toad's trouble. Ah, well, let's get this wheel on.'

After more heaving under Ratty's skilled direction, the caravan was once more upright and on four wheels. That done, they set about cleaning it, and before long it was restored to its pristine glory.

A week or so later, Ratty and Mole returned, provisions in hand, to prepare the caravan for their promised trip. 'Oh, Ratty,' Mole remarked enthusiastically as they neared it, 'I am so looking forward to a caravan trip!'

'Yes, I must say, Mole, that, while an open road will never match a flowing river, I feel a need to travel. It's in the air, see . . .' He broke off, when he saw a line of Fieldmice sitting on the ground beside the caravan with their bags and suitcases.

'Oh, hullo!'

'Good morning, Mr Mole! Good morning, Mr Rat!' they

chorused in reply. 'We thought we'd wait – to say "goodbye" and "thank you".'

'Enjoyed your stay, have you?' Mole inquired.

'It's the nicest home that ever was, Mr Mole!'

'Good, good!' Rat approved. 'So where are you making your new home, eh?' he added.

There was an uneasy pause.

'Look here – you have *found* a new place?' Ratty asked, suspecting that the shy animals, so grateful for the help given to them earlier, might have decided to move on without knowing what awaited them. Mole looked over his glasses, and added, gently, '*Have* you got somewhere?'

'Well ... not exactly, Mr Mole.'

'Yes or no?' Rat said, more firmly.

'Erm ... no,' sighed one of the mice.

'Oh, my gosh! Oh, Ratty!' Mole exclaimed, touched both by the Fieldmice's plight and their reluctance to burden others with it.

Rat was already considering what to do: 'Look here, Mole, old fellow – we can't turn these Fieldmice out so we can have a holiday! They'll be snug and safe here, and after all, we *have* our homes ...'

The Rat wondered how to stop the Fieldmice feeling uneasy at accepting further help. 'Look here, you fellows – we ... we only dropped by to tell you that it's off,' he said. 'We won't be going! Important business, and ... er ...'

Mole fell in with his friend's deception, and interrupted: 'That's right! So ...'

'... so you needn't go!' finished Rat.

'You mean that we can stay, Mr Rat? That this can always be our home?' said the delighted Fieldmice. Rat and Mole nodded.

'Oh, thank you!' The mice chorused their thanks.

But Rat suddenly frowned. 'There's only one thing, Mole.'

'What's that, Ratty?'

'Toad! He has been going on about the caravan ...'

'Oh dear!' Mole wondered. 'What if he insists ...'

'Oh, Mole!' The Rat was seized by doubt. 'Perhaps I was too hasty. Perhaps I should have ...'

Mole was not going to give up, however: 'But if we explain to him how things are ... If we tell him ...' he began, only to stop, when distracted by a tinkling noise. 'Ratty! What's that?'

'I don't know, Mole. It sounds like ...'

And it was. A bicycle bell – attached to a bicycle, astride which sat ... Toad!

'Ring-a-ding! Ring-a-ding! Ring-a-ding! Oh, for the life a-wheel!' sang the ebullient creature as he rolled into view.

Toad shuddered to a halt next to them. 'My dear friends, what joys I have discovered! The finest bicycle that ever was! Such silent, swooping speed! Such hills surmounted, valleys conquered!'

'Oh Toad. Not another craze!' said the Rat, resignedly.

'Craze! This is but the beginning of a *lifetime's* bliss! Ah, the swift velocipede!'

'Oh, Toad!' Ratty attempted to quell Toad's torrent of enthusiasm – to no avail.

'... the fresh air streaming past one's face. The whirling kaleidoscope of villages ...'

'Toad! Do be quiet!' Ratty shouted in desperation.

'Oh, I say!'

'I thought you wanted to go on a caravan trip!' Rat continued.

'Pooh! Caravan! A snail's home on wheels! A horse-drawn dog's-kennel! A mere ...'

'Yes, yes, all right, Toad!' Rat burst in again. 'Am I to take it then that you will *not* be going on a caravan trip?'

For once, Toad realized that his vacillation might irritate his friends, prepared as they evidently were for another trip.

'Oh, Ratty, Mole – Oh, forgive me – but I *cannot* come! I hear the "ping" of chain-guards, the ring of bells! I hear . . .'

'*Thank*-you Toad!' said Mole, firmly. 'So the Fieldmice can stay here for a while?'

'Here! Fieldmice? Oh yes – forever! No *caravan* is swift enough to match *my* spirit! And now, dear friends, I must be on my

way! The four-spring patent saddle shall bear me hence! Ting-a-ling! Farewell!'

'My word, he's got it awfully bad!'

'As ever, Mole!' Rat agreed.

'Still, the Fieldmice have a home!' Mole continued, brightening.

'Yes, yes. It's an ill wind that blows nobody any good, and I must say . . . !'

'Morning all!' said a deep voice cheerfully behind them. It was Alfred. And he, thought Rat, would be raring to go. They had forgotten all about him!

'Look, Alfred,' Rat began, 'there's been a change of plan! I'm sorry ...'

'How did you know that?' Alfred didn't seem downcast – more surprised.

Mole was puzzled. 'How d'you mean, Alfred, "How do *we* know?" How do *you* know?'

'Seeing as 'ow it's me who's 'ad to change it ...'

'*You*?' began Mole. 'But *we* ...'

'It's the 'arvester,' Alfred explained. 'Broken down it has! Blew up it has! Ha, ha! The farmer's real mad! So he 'as to turn to me, like. I'm ... sorry to spoil your plans!'

'Not at all, Alfred! Not at all!' Mole said, smiling inwardly.

As Alfred trotted off to work, muttering about new-fangled rubbish, Mole turned to Rat. 'Well! So that's all right! Toad doesn't care, Alfred can't come, the Fieldmice have a home, and we ...' He hesitated, a little sad at losing the prospect he'd been so looking forward to.

'... we have our homes to go to!' said Rat brightly, then added, 'Wouldn't fancy a day on the river, I suppose?'

'Oh, Ratty!' said Mole, contentedly.

THE GRAND ANNUAL SHOW

It was summer. The first freshness of the season, of green grass and dew-laden mornings, was over. Harvest-time was coming once more. The excitement of gathering in the fruits, of making sure for winter, would reach everyone soon. But today it was only the dishes that Mole had gathered – after breakfast in the neat, hidden cosiness of Mole End. He felt that the effort might have earned him a sit-down and a cup of tea, when ... clatter, slither, plop. A letter! Letters didn't come often to Mole End. Who could it be from? Not Badger, thought Mole. He was sociable enough once you got to know him – but he hardly ever *wrote* to anyone. And it couldn't be Toad – the paper wasn't *half* fancy enough. Mole savoured the uncertainty a moment more . . . then opened it . . . and read.

'Oh my, Oh my!' he exclaimed. 'How wonderful to win . . . ! But then, of course, I never would . . .'

A letter arrived at Toad Hall, too, and it woke Toad. He sat up in bed.

'Post!' he announced to himself cheerfully. 'Letters from

admirers! An invitation from the Palace . . . !' Having eventually overcome the indignity, as he saw it, of having to fetch his own post, Toad clambered back into his ancestral four-poster, opened the envelope, and read the letter with almost as much delight as if it *had* been from the Palace . . . .

Badger, on the other hand, had been out for a walk, bright and early as usual. When he returned, he found one of the young rabbits standing by his front door, examining a letter. The Rabbit didn't see Badger until the last moment, and he started guiltily:

'Oh! Er . . . 'morning, Mr Badger! Been out for your morning stroll, Sir?'

'I have,' said Badger, heavily.

'Missed the postman, Sir!'

'Hmmm! But you, I see, did not! Off home with you!'

'Er ... ycs, Mr Badger,' muttered the thankful Rabbit, handing over the letter and scampering off.

'Hmph!' remarked Badger to himself. 'Better see what it says, I suppose.'

Now, as you may have guessed, all these letters were the same, and Ratty too was about to get onc. When he heard the rattle of his letter box, he put aside the copy of the *Tatler* he was reading, and eagerly opened the envelope.

'Dear Field, River or Wild Wood Folk,' he read, *'this year, as usual, we are going to hold our Grand Annual Show* – Oh, splendid – *but with the additional attraction of a special Silver Cup, generously donated by Mrs M. F. H. Carrington-Moss, J. P., which will be awarded for the Best-of-Show in any class.*

'I say! What fun!' Ratty exclaimed to himself. He'd have time to bake one of his special walnut cakes! He thought for a moment more:

'I wonder if the others have had an invitation too?'

There were several jars of blackcurrant jelly on the table in Mole's kitchen, and he was just standing back with a little sigh of satisfaction when he noticed that the handle of the spoon was still sticky. He tried to lick the jelly off.

'Oh, bother!' Somehow, some of it had contrived to get on his glasses. He put the spoon down on the table – and, just too late, realized he'd put it on the recipe. 'Oh, now look what I've done!'

He took off his glasses to polish them on the edge of his apron, but the jelly was *so* sticky that it just smeared.

'Oh! Bother blackcurrant jelly! And bother the Silver Cup!'

And just at this tiresome moment, there was a knock at the door.

'Oh, blow! Come in! Come in!' said Mole, a little flustered.

It was Rat. 'I say, Mole, old chap, what are you up to?'

'Oh, Ratty! Why did I ever think I could ...?' Mole broke off, near to tears of frustration.

'Could what, old fellow?'

'Could make blackcurrant jelly, could enter it for Best-of-Show, could win the Cup!'

'Now, now, old chap! It *smells* glorious! It looks splendid!' Rat wiped his finger along the spoon handle, which

was still sitting provocatively on the table, and tried a little. 'Mmmm! Mmmm! It *tastes* wonderful!'

'Does it?' Mole ventured.

'It tastes like ... like summer days, and autumn hedgerows, and winter tea-cakes ... all rolled into one!' Rat enthused.

'Goodness, Ratty!' said a disbelieving but delighted Mole. 'Do you really think so?'

'I *do* really think so,' replied Rat. 'Shouldn't think my walnut cake will stand a chance.'

'Your walnut cake?' Mole was intrigued. 'You ... you don't mean you're going in for Best-of-Show too?'

Rat, like the modest fellow he was, hadn't foreseen Mole's interest in his, Ratty's, entry, and was a little embarrassed at the prospect of admitting his earlier enthusiasm for the competition. So he replied, a little self-deprecatingly: 'Well, only for the fun of it. I don't much care about winning Best-of-Show Silver Cup – but, yes!'

Mole could sense his friend's discomfort: 'Oh, I don't *care* about it. I just thought I ought to join in.'

'Exactly,' agreed Rat, appreciating Mole's sensitivity. 'Er ...

you ... uh ... you don't have any *walnuts*, I suppose?'

'Oh dear! I never keep them, Ratty. They disagree with me. But Badger does! He gathers them in the Wild Wood. He told me so.'

'Well, good old Badger! Might pop along and pay him a visit then.'

Mole needed only a little encouragement to abandon his work. He'd had enough of kitchens, ... and pans ... and jam!

'Ooh! Can I come?' he exclaimed.

Rat and Mole found Badger in his kitchen – stabbing walnuts with a needle! Rat had timed his visit perfectly. He inquired if Badger had any to spare, and Badger replied, stabbing as he did so, 'Take as many ... walnuts as you ... need, my dear fellow! You can see I've ... plenty.' As he said 'plenty', Badger's concentration lapsed a little, and the next stab caught his thumb. Mole was naturally at first concerned that the Badger had hurt himself, but the injury was clearly not serious, and Mole began to wonder about Badger's earnest determination.

'Oh dear! Oh dear!' he voiced. 'Er ... Badger ... not that it's any of my business – but *why* are you stabbing those walnuts?'

'Going to pickle 'em, Mole, my boy!'

He paused, then added nonchalantly, 'Besides, I might just enter a jar of 'em in the Annual Show, if I can be bothered. *If* I enter, it will be merely to support a local event!'

'Ah, yes! Of course!' said the Rat, suspecting that even Badger might be pleased if he won. But Badger dispelled such unjust questioning of his motives by adding, darkly, 'And to keep an eye on others, who might see the Annual Show as an opportunity for showing off, like ...'

'Toad!' Rat and Mole joined in. Rat could see that Badger had been his usual perceptive self and so they set off to pay a 'social call' on Toad Hall.

Toad was preparing his entry for the Show with his usual skill, patience, application, and modesty. On the table in the Great Hall, he was putting into practice his vision, a culmination of his extensive reading of *Great Wines of the World* and his exhaustive knowledge of chemistry imparted by years – well, days, anyway – of dedicated experimentation with his 'Chemistry Set No. 3'. All his equipment, both intellectual and practical, would now come to fruition in a prize-winning vintage. Toad had no *audience*, but why should that prevent a recital of his skills?

'This is the way to make wine! *Cotes de Beaunes*? Pooh! *Mouton Cadet*. Hoo hoo hoo! Oh chemistry! Oh *Toad*! You clever, clever Toad! You Isaac Newton of a Toad! And the world will hear a new name, a great name: *Vin Spectaculaire de Chateau Toad!*'

And he sang a new verse of his song:

As the Bishop sipped the nectar,
His cheeks with pleasure glowed,
'Who makes this wond'rous wine,' he asked –
They answered 'Mr Toad!'
De dumm, de dumm, de doo-doo . . .

'Hoo, hoo! Bubble away, my miracle! Soon the world will be knocking at my door!'

Just as Toad said 'Door', there was a loud knock, for Badger, Ratty and Mole had arrived.

'Good heavens! *Already*!' said the astonished though delighted Toad. 'Ah, well! Genius will out!'

He went to welcome his visitors, musing upon who might have reacted so quickly. 'Oh, Oh, it's you!' he said when he saw them, scarcely concealing his disappointment.

'It is, Toad!' said Badger heavily. 'Who were you expecting?'

'Well, I thought ... that is, I was expecting ... well – come in, come in! Is it about the Special Silver Cup?'

'Heavens, Toad!' Mole exclaimed, 'how *do* you know?'

'Oh ... inevitable, my dear fellow,' said Toad, airily indicating the wine-making equipment. 'All that ... chemistry ... the wonders of science ... my *genius*! Well, it was bound to get about. I've er ... you know, saved a place for it on the mantelpiece.'

'Saved a place ...' began Rat, incredulous.

'*One* moment, Toad!' Badger interrupted, with the verbal counterpart of a hand on Toad's shoulder. 'Am I to understand that you believe you have as good as won the Best-of-Show award?'

'Well, yes, of course!' Toad said, confident as ever, adding in an aside to Rat, 'I do so hate false modesty, don't you?'

Badger continued doggedly. 'And for *what* have you as good as won it, Toad?'

'Hmmm? Oh, for my wine! For my home-brewed elderflower wine!'

Each listening animal took in this astonishing conceit – astonishing even by Toad's standards – and each reacted in his characteristic way:

'Oh, Toad!' said Mole, disapprovingly. Ratty had a slight edge to his voice as he said, 'Oh, really, Toad!' Badger adopted his most severe and gruff tone, and said: 'Toad! You are a wretched, conceited, self-deceiving animal!' But such admonishment was lost on Toad, who remained utterly sure of his skills:

'No, not at all, my dear Badger! My wine will simply be the best in the world! It is the work of genius, it is!'

'It is altogether too much!' Badger interposed. 'Come on Rat! Let us leave this miserable animal to drown in his own conceit!'

Badger led the way, and Toad was left alone to remark to himself, 'Ha! Well, really! Ha! Tut! Jealousy does terrible things to a chap. Envy of my chemical genius ...'

As he spoke, though, the bubbling noises coming from the Hall changed from a friendly burble to an angry, ominous rattling. 'I say! I wonder why it's making that funny noise? Perhaps I ought to ...' Toad turned towards the Hall but – perhaps fortunately *before* he could reach the apparatus – there was a fearful explosion. When at last the smoke cleared, Toad was rather less dapper than his usual self, and the apparatus was little more than shimmering fragments of glass.

Such was Toad's temperament that disasters like this were instantly expressed in a torrent of self-pity:

> 'Oh! Oh, horror, Oh, despair! Dreams ... shattered!
> Ambitions ... cast down!
> Suit ... absolutely ruined!
> No more chemistry! No *Chateau Toad Hall*!
> No Silver Cup!'

But even as he bewailed his misfortune, a sly look came over his face, and with, if the truth be told, a less-than-honourable thought in his mind, he set off for his wine cellar.

On the day of the show, the four friends were well satisfied. Each won his class. Even the Weasels had their success, and whilst some might not rejoice that it was so, one had to admit that their pumpkin was a most handsome fruit. Mole, in his generous way, remarked so to Badger: 'I say, haven't they done well?'

Then at last the moment came for the Best-of-Show. Mrs Carrington-Moss took the floor: 'The judges were quite unanimous in agreeing with me that, without doubt, the Best-of-Show Award of the Special Silver Cup goes to the Weasels' Wild Wood allotment Society – 'Oh shame!' – for their

PICKLED
WALNUT
SEPT 1909
T.E. BADGER
PICKLED
WALNUT
SEPT 1909
T.E. BADGER
1st

magnificent pumpkin. So, without more ado, and before I present the Cup, let me decorate the winning entry in the appropriate way.'

And she leaned forward to pin the rosette on the pumpkin. The result was extraordinary, for there was consternation among the Weasels – scarcely the reaction one would expect from proud prizewinners:

''Ere, lady! Knock it off!'

'No, no, no! Don't stick the . . .'

But she did – and there was a loud hissing as the pumpkin shrank and crumpled. It was a painted blown-up bladder!

There was a gasp from the crowd, and Mrs Carrington-Moss stiffened.

'I see!' she admonished.

Even the Weasels were shamefaced at their unmasking.

'I wonder if our ... er ... if our bikes is all right?' said one.

'Eh?' replied his neighbour. 'We never came on no bi ... Ah!' And they fled from the disapproving stare of the crowd.

'Well, in that case,' Mrs Carrington-Moss continued, 'We shall award the Best-of-Show to the Elderflower Wine entered by Mr Toad.'

Toad accepted this as only his rightful due:

'Hurray! Quite right! Genius will out! Well done, old girl!'

'Oh, not Toad!' exclaimed the Rat. 'He'll be insufferable!'

'*Will* be? Huh!' Badger retorted.

Toad, indeed, was glorying in his success.

'Have a glass of wine, Mrs ... er ... Mrs Thingy! I give you a toast ...' Toad held his bottle aloft. But he didn't notice that the label had slipped, unstuck by its time in the wet ice-bucket. And beneath the label could be read another, less home-made one: '*Niederhauser Herrmanshole Spatlese*' it read.

Mrs Carrington-Moss caught sight of it, and finished his toast for him, although not in quite the tone he had expected: 'Toad!'

'Yes?'

'I have that wine in my cellar!'

'Well, you needn't think I pinched it! *This* wine is from *my* cellar! And I . . . I . . .' He became aware that the approving chatter from the crowds around had changed to a *dis*approving mutter, and his voice tailed away.

'Oh . . . Toad!' said Ratty, Mole and Badger together, half sad at their friend's folly, half angry at this blatant conceit.

For once, Toad agreed with the Weasels as to the best course of action. 'I wonder if those poor fellows have found their bicycle?' he remarked, sidling away from the prize-giving.

In the silence which followed, voices were heard from outside the tent. It was the Fieldmice. 'Hang on! Wait! Wait for us!' And they tottered in, struggling with a huge marrow.

'Sorry we're late! We had to *carry* it all the way after the wheelbarrow collapsed! Have we missed the judging?'

'On the contrary!' Mrs Carrington-Moss replied, admiringly. 'You are just in time to receive the award for Best-of-Show!'

This was a very popular choice. The crowds cheered, and Rat remarked:

'Well done, young 'uns! Put us *all* in our places!'

'And a good thing too!' added Badger. 'Now I think we'd better follow Toad home. There are a few things I have to say to that unfortunate animal!'

They found a contrite Toad sobbing in Toad Hall:

'I can't think what came over me!'

'Just what always comes over you, Toad,' said Rat.

'Yes ...' Badger thrust in quickly, 'greed, conceit, stupidity, lack of consideration.'

'I say! Steady on, Badger!' Toad complained.

But Badger continued: 'I should never have let you take part in a competition. It brings out the worst in all of us.'

'Oh, you're so right, my dear wise old Badger! Never again shall I flaunt my skills as a wine-maker!'

'Oh, Toady!' Mole cried, admiring such determination from his friend.

Even Rat had to show his approval: 'Yes, well ... er ... good chap, Toad!' But he spoke too soon, for Toad added irrepressibly:

'But come and have a look at my cauliflower!'

'Oh, Toad!'

'Yes! It's a miracle of science! Wait 'til next year – I'll give 'em pumpkins! I'll give 'em vegetable marrows ...'

Ratty, Badger and Mole could only look at one another, aghast.